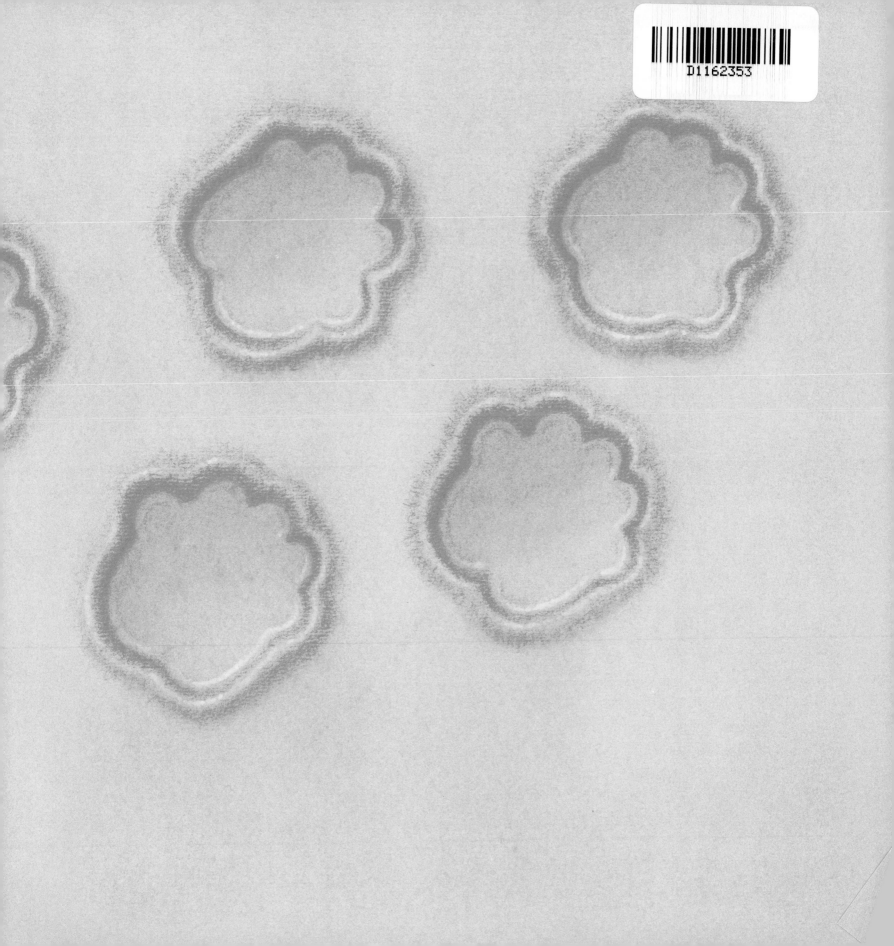

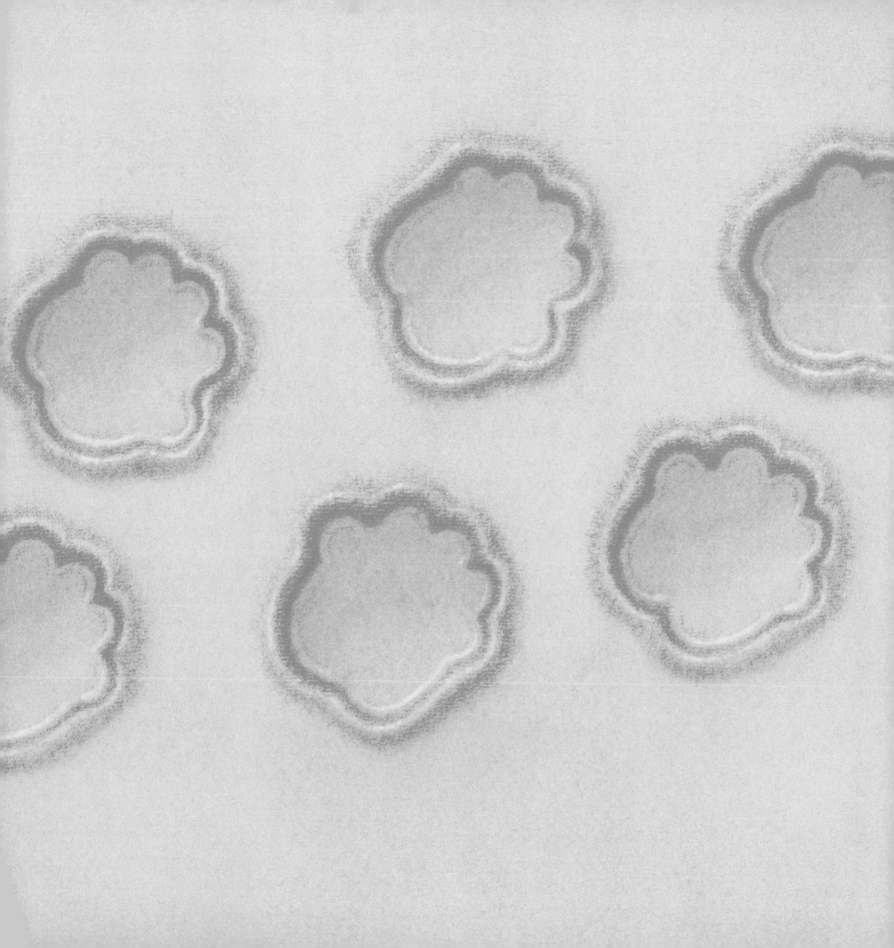

FIONA,
IT'S BEDTIME

NEW YORK TIMES BESTSELLING ILLUSTRATOR
RICHARD COWDREY

For Cindy
—RC

ZONDERKIDZ

Fiona, It's Bedtime
Copyright © 2020 by Zondervan
Illustrations © 2020 by Zondervan

Requests for information should be addressed to:

Zonderkidz, 3900 Sparks Drive SE,
Grand Rapids, Michigan 49546

Library of Congress Cataloging-in-Publication Data

Names: Cowdrey, Richard, illustrator.
   Title: Fiona, It's bedtime, / illustrated by Richard Cowdrey ;
contributors,
   Barbara Herndon, Mary Hassinger, Katelyn Van Kooten.
   Other titles: Fiona, It's bedtime
   Description: Grand Rapids, Michigan : Zonderkidz, [2020]
| Summary: At the end of a busy day, Fiona the hippo wishes
goodnight to all of her friends at the zoo. |
   Identifiers: LCCN 2019013998 (print) | LCCN 2019018036
(ebook) | ISBN 9780310767701 () | ISBN 9780310767558 (hard-
cover)
   Subjects: | CYAC: Stories in rhyme. | Bedtime--Fiction. | Hip-
popotamus--Fiction. | Zoo animals--Fiction. | Animals--Fiction.
   Classification: LCC PZ8.3.C83415 (ebook) | LCC
PZ8.3.C83415 lt 2020 (print) |
   DDC [E]--dc23

   LC record available at https://lccn.loc.gov/2019013998

Illustrated by: Richard Cowdrey
Contributors: : Barbara Herndon, Mary Hassinger, Katelyn Van Kooten
Design: Cindy Davis and Kris Nelson

Printed in China

HOWL! HOWL! Hoot Hoot

Gobble Gobble

ROAR! GRRRR

HOWL! ROAR! SQUAWK! COO!
The sun is setting at the zoo.
The critters had a busy day
filled with laughter, fun, and play.

SQUAWK! SQUAWK!

But now it's bedtime at the zoo.
It's bedtime for Fiona too.
Before today's adventure ends,
She'll say "GOOD NIGHT" to all her friends.

GOOD NIGHT, Koala, time to doze
with your paws curled up near your nose.
Safe and happy in the trees,
snoozing in the evening breeze.

GOOD NIGHT, Cheetah, lightning-fast,
now it's time for sleep at last.
Snuggle up in Mama's fur
and drift off to her loving purr.

GOOD NIGHT, Tortoise—where's your head?
Ooh, tucked inside your shell-shaped bed.
It's warm and snug, so settle in
and let your reptile dreams begin.

GOOD NIGHT, Sloth, to bed you go,
moving v-e-r-y, v-e-r-y slow.
Sleepy eyes and big sloth yawn,
sweet dreams till the break of dawn.

GOOD NIGHT, flamingos, on your toes.
You sleep in such a silly pose!
Please make a promise that you'll keep—
don't fall down while you're asleep.

GOOD NIGHT, otters, in a row,
hand-in-hand and toe-to-toe.
Drift to sleep. Rock and sway.
Together, you won't float away.

GOOD NIGHT, meerkats, in a heap.
It's time for you to go to sleep.
Cuddled up and all piled high,
now dream beneath the starry sky.

GOOD NIGHT, giraffes, as tall as trees.
Time to bend your knobby knees.
It's a long way to the ground.
Now rest your heads and settle down.

GOOD NIGHT, tigers, filled with pride.
You curl up in the grass to hide.
It's time to let out one last roar,
and then a grumbly, growly snore.

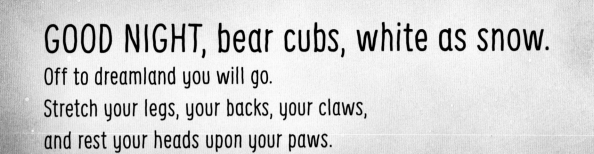

GOOD NIGHT, bear cubs, white as snow.
Off to dreamland you will go.
Stretch your legs, your backs, your claws,
and rest your heads upon your paws.

GOOD NIGHT, wolf and sleepy pack.

GOOD NIGHT, apes on Mama's back.

GOOD NIGHT, wildebeest and gnu.

GOOD NIGHT, huddled penguins too.

GOOD NIGHT, Lizard. No more creeping.

GOOD NIGHT, Zebra, standing sleeping.

GOOD NIGHT, Lion, mane so sleek.

GOOD NIGHT, Toucan. Rest your beak.

YAWN! SNORE! SIGH! COO!
The moon shines down upon the zoo.
All GOOD NIGHTS have now been said.

Fiona?...

YAWN!

SNORE!

SIGH!

COO!
COO!

Time to go to bed.

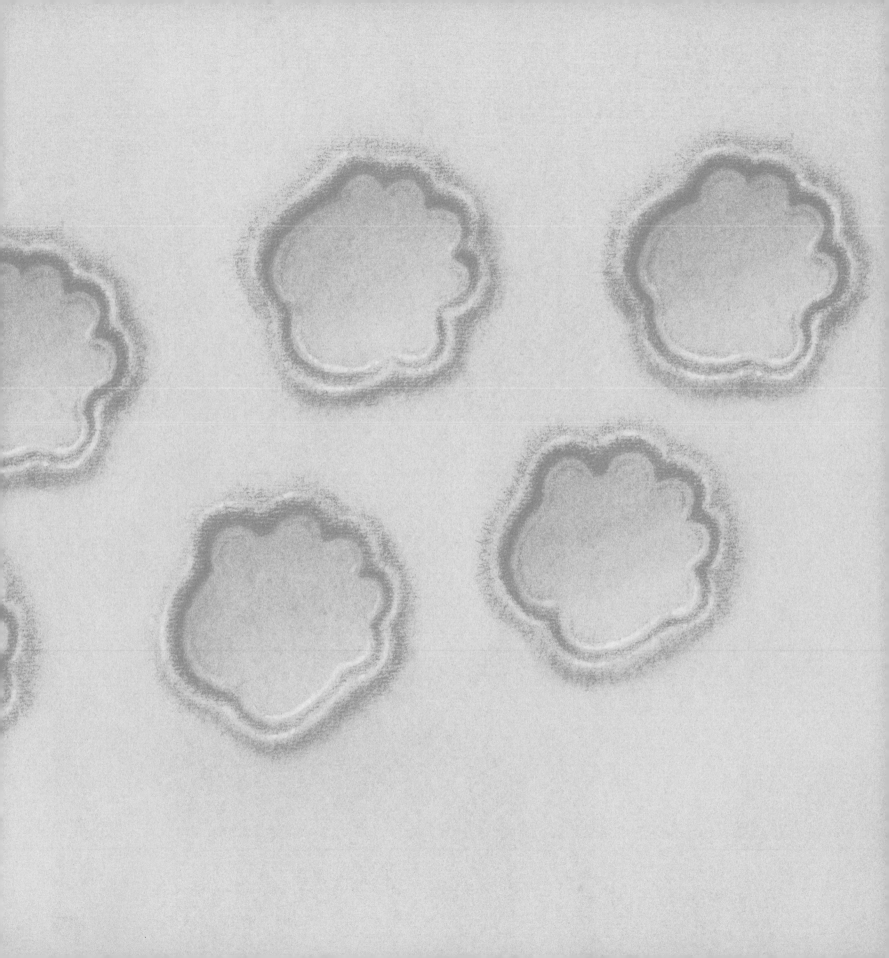

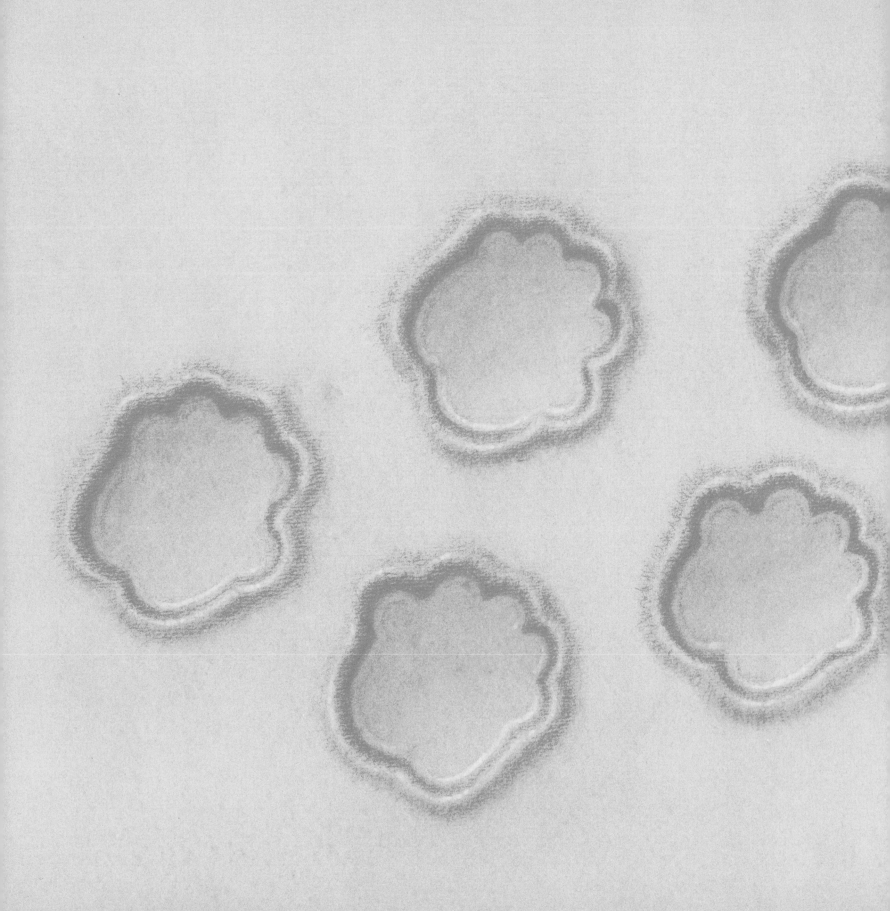